America's Game
Houston
Astros

CHRIS W. SEHNERT

ABDO & Daughters
PUBLISHING

Published by Abdo & Daughters, 4940 Viking Dr., Suite 622, Edina, MN 55435.

Cover photo: Allsport
Interior photos: Allsport, page 5.
　　　　　Wide World Photo, pages 1, 6, 8, 9, 11-13, 15-17, 21, 25, 27, 28.

Edited by Paul Joseph

Library of Congress Cataloging–in–Publication Data

Sehnert, Chris W.
　　Houston Astros / Chris W. Sehnert
　　　　p. cm. — (America's game)
　　Includes index.
　　Summary: Focuses on key players and events in the history of the Houston Astros, the first major league baseball team to play their home games indoors.
　　ISBN　1-56239-669-2
　　1. Houston Astros (Baseball team)—History—Juvenile literature.
[1. Houston Astros (Baseball team) 2. Baseball—History.]
I. Title. II. Series.
GV875.H64S45　1997
796.357'64'097641411—dc20
　　　　　　　　　　　　　　　　　　　96-22378
　　　　　　　　　　　　　　　　　　　　CIP
　　　　　　　　　　　　　　　　　　　　AC

Contents

Houston Astros

The Houston Astros were the first Major League Baseball team to play their home games indoors. They moved into the Houston Astrodome in 1965. As they continue through their fourth decade of play, the Astros are seeking their first National League (NL) Pennant.

The Houston franchise has suffered through more than their share of misfortune: blood-sucking insects, a field of dead grass, blinding glare, and dumbfounding player trades. They have even managed to lose a game in which their pitcher threw a no-hitter.

Throwing no-hitters is actually a tradition for the Astros. Among their all-time great players was Nolan Ryan. The tall Texan threw more hitless games than anyone else in baseball history.

Today, the Astros are preparing for blast off with some of the brightest young stars baseball has to offer. Craig Biggio and Jeff Bagwell lead Houston into a future where the sky is no longer the limit.

Facing Page: Jeff Bagwell, the Astros' power-hitting first baseman, was the first Houston player to win the NL MVP Award in 1994.

Colt .45s

Houston, Texas, has been home to professional baseball since 1888. Prior to the 1960s, however, only minor league teams existed in the "Lone Star State." Dizzy Dean and Tris Speaker began their playing days with the Houston Buffaloes before going on to Hall-of-Fame careers in the "big leagues." When the National League voted to expand, Texas was rewarded with its first major league franchise.

Houston's new team was originally named the Colt .45s, after the famous pistol that helped win the West. Along with the New York Mets, they began play in 1962. The Colt .45s played their first three seasons in the hastily constructed Colt Stadium.

Roy Hofheinz was the original owner of the Houston franchise. He had hoped to open the team's inaugural season in a park to be named the Harris County Domed Stadium. When problems in construction delayed the project, the Colt .45s were forced to play in the outdoor facility built next door. High heat and humidity, combined with swarms of blood-sucking insects, earned the park its nickname, "Mosquito Heaven."

The expansion draft left the Colt .45s and General Manager Paul Richards with very few quality players to pick from. They finished eighth in 1962, ahead of the Chicago Cubs and New York Mets. Cuban-born Roman Mejias cracked 24 home runs (HRs), putting together his finest season in the majors. The next season, Mejias was sent to the Boston Red Sox.

The only thing keeping the Colts out of the NL cellar the next two seasons were their expansion brothers, the equally pathetic Mets.

Facing Page: Nellie Fox joined the Colt .45s in 1964 as player-manager.

Rusty Staub began his 23-year major league career with Houston in 1963. The one bright spot for the Colts that season was Don Nottebart's no-hitter over the Philadelphia Phillies. With an incredibly low team batting average of .220, Houston pitchers could hardly do less if they expected to win.

Houston was only slightly better in their final season outdoors in 1964. Nellie Fox joined the Colt .45s that season as a player-coach. Fox had played under Paul Richards as a member of the Chicago White Sox in the 1950s. He led American League (AL) second basemen in fielding average six times in his career. Nellie was an AL All-Star 12 times. He ended his 19-year playing career with Houston in 1965.

Hal Woodeshick led NL relief pitchers with 23 saves in 1964. However, he and Fox could not save the Colt .45s from another ninth-place finish. After three years and countless mosquito bites, Houston's new indoor stadium was finally ready for action in 1965. The Colt .45s hung up their spurs and prepared for the future, with a brand new identity.

Left: Rusty Staub joined the Colts in 1963, beginning a 23-year career in the major leagues.

Left: A fisheye view of the new Houston Astrodome in 1965.

"Houston. . . We Have A Problem"

In the early 1960s, the Mercury space missions sent the first American astronauts into orbit around the Earth. Mission Control for NASA (National Aeronautics and Space Administration) was located in Houston, Texas. In honor of the space program, baseball's first indoor stadium was named the Houston Astrodome. The team that moved within changed their name from the Colt .45s to the Houston Astros.

The Astrodome was originally built with a glass roof, allowing the sun to shine through on the natural grass inside. Unfortunately, while this feature added to the space-age appearance of the structure, it also caused problems. Light reflecting off the glass panels caused blinding glare, making even the easiest of fly balls difficult to catch. The grass began to die before the 1965 home opener.

In an exhibition game with the New York Yankees, Mickey Mantle launched the first Astrodome homer. The new surroundings were of little help to the Astros when it came to winning. Houston finished the season just in front of the last-place New York Mets for the third straight time.

Before the 1966 season, several options were explored to fix the Astrodome's problems. By this time, the only thing keeping the grass green was a regular coating of paint. Likewise, fitting each player with a special set of sunglasses didn't seem to be the best alternative. Finally, the ceiling of clear glass was replaced with opaque panels. The field was covered with a new invention made of green nylon. The synthetic grass became commonly known as Astroturf.

One of the first players to master the art of fielding on the new surface was Houston's second baseman, Joe Morgan. Batted balls, which on natural grass would have been routine grounders, turned into skipping bullets on Astroturf. Many charging infielders were rendered helpless, as one-hoppers went soaring over their heads.

Joe Morgan was a native Texan, who began his career with the Colt .45s in 1963. He made his first All-Star appearance as a member of the Houston Astros in 1970. Two years later, Morgan was traded to the Cincinnati Reds, where he blossomed into one of the greatest second basemen of all time.

With all of the frustration and problems the Astrodome caused in its first two years, its many innovations have been long lasting. Giant replay flashing scoreboards and luxury suites are but two of the ideas originated in Houston's "Eighth Wonder of the World." The benefit of low maintenance has made Astroturf the surface of choice in stadiums across the country. Domes of all shapes and sizes have since popped up wherever inclement weather prevails.

Facing page: Joe Morgan began his career in Houston.

Astros' No-Hitters

W hen the Colt .45s' Don Nottebart no-hit the Philadelphia Phillies on May 17, 1963, he started a Texas tradition. The San Francisco Giants' Juan Marichal returned the favor, no-hitting Houston that same season. In 1964, Houston's Ken Johnson no-hit the Cincinnati Reds. Johnson wound up losing the game 1-0 when he and Nellie Fox made a pair of ninth-inning errors. In their first 25 major league seasons, the Houston franchise was involved in 10 no-hit decisions!

The first no-hitter involving the team known as the Houston Astros came on June 18, 1967. Don Wilson performed the trick, defeating the Atlanta Braves 2-0. It was the third no-hit game pitched by a Houston player, but it was only their first "no-no" (allowing no hits and no runs).

The Astros received strong offensive production from outfielders Rusty Staub (.333 batting average) and Jim Wynn (37 HRs, 107 RBIs) in 1967. Wynn was nicknamed "the Toy Cannon" for his small size (5' 9", 170 lbs.) and powerful bat. Houston completed the season with their usual ninth-place finish, just in front of the last-place New York Mets.

Left: Astros' outfielder Jim Wynn.

12

For Houston, 1968 was truly a season to forget. The Mets finally gave up the NL basement, and the Astros moved in. The next season the NL expanded for the second time in the decade, adding the Montreal Expos and San Diego Padres. Divisional play was set up that season, and the Astros became members of the NL West.

On April 30, 1969, Cincinnati's Jim Maloney pitched the third no-hitter of his career, defeating the Astros 10-0. The very next day, Don Wilson answered with his second no-no, as the Astros beat the

Don Wilson celebrates after pitching a no-hitter against the Atlanta Braves in 1967.

Reds 4-0. Wilson nearly got a third no-hitter of his own in 1974. He had pitched eight innings without allowing a hit, when he was lifted for a pinch-hitter.

The 1969 baseball season was culminated by the New York Mets' miraculous World Championship. Among the Mets' tremendous pitching staff that season was a fireballing Texan named Nolan Ryan. The career of Ryan would last 27 seasons, in which he set an all-time record for no-hitters with 7. The fifth of Nolan's peerless performances came as a member of the Houston Astros. It was a no-no over the Los Angeles Dodgers (5-0) on September 26, 1981.

The three remaining Astro no-hitters were performed by Larry Dierker, Ken Forsch, and Mike Scott. Dierker's career highlight came in the last full season of his major league career. He no-hit the Montreal Expos on July 9, 1976. Forsch's no-no was over the Atlanta Braves, on April 7, 1979. His older brother, Bob Forsch, completed two no-hitters for the St. Louis Cardinals.

Finally, when Mike Scott no-hit the San Francisco Giants on September 25, 1986, he clinched the NL West Division Title for the Houston Astros. On the 25th anniversary of the Houston franchise, what better way could there have been to celebrate?

Facing page: Nolan Ryan threw one of his seven career no-hitters while pitching for the Houston Astros in 1981.

Cesar Cedeno sweeps across the plate to steal home in a 1977 game against the Chicago Cubs.

Dis-Astros!

In 1969, the Houston Astros had as many wins as losses (81-81). For the first time in franchise history, they finished out of the ranks of losing ballclubs. The optimism didn't last long, however, as the Astros began another descent the following season. In 1975, they finished with their worst record ever (64-97). For Houston, bad luck, along with some awful player trades, made the 1970s a decade of disaster.

Cesar Cedeno made his debut with the Astros in 1970. He was from the Dominican Republic. Houston scouts spotted his talent, and signed him to a contract when he was 16 years old. Cedeno's overwhelming baseball skills immediately led people to compare him to Hall-of-Fame players Henry Aaron, Willie Mays, and Roberto Clemente. As a 19-year-old rookie, Cedeno looked as if he would prove them right.

In his first four seasons with the Astros, Cedeno led the NL in doubles twice, won two Gold Glove Awards as an outfielder, and became an NL All-Star. The Astrodome was nicknamed "Cesar's Palace." Then, on December 11, 1973, disaster struck the life of the young Astro star.

Cesar Cedeno was charged with the murder of his girlfriend in his hometown of Santo Domingo. He was later released on reduced charges of involuntary manslaughter when it was proven that Altagracia de la Cruz had accidentally killed herself with his pistol. Cedeno returned to play 13 more seasons in the major leagues. He never reached his projected potential.

In 1969, Houston General Manager "Spec" Richardson traded Mike Cuellar to the Baltimore Orioles. The Cuban pitcher went on to win 125 ball games over the next five seasons, leading Baltimore to three straight World Series appearances (1969-1971). Richardson repeated his gaffe in 1972, sending Joe Morgan, Cesar Geronimo,

Astros' pitcher Joe Niekro delivers his knuckleball pitch in a game against the New York Mets in 1983.

Houston

Nellie Fox was an AL All-Star 12 times during his 19-year playing career.

Joe Morgan made his first All-Star appearance as an Astro in 1963.

Don Wilson pitched the first of his three no-hitters in 1967 against the Atlanta Braves.

In 1979, Joe Niekro had 21 wins, tying him for the lead with his brother Phil, who threw for the Atlanta Braves.

Astros

All-Star pitcher J.R. Richard led the NL in strikeouts in 1978 (303) and 1979 (313).

As an Astro in 1981, Nolan Ryan pitched the fifth of his seven career no-hitters.

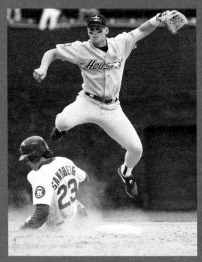

Craig Biggio was the NL's All-Star catcher in 1991, and the NL's All-Star second baseman in 1992.

In 1994, Jeff Bagwell was the Astros' first player to win the NL MVP Award.

and Jack Billingham to the Cincinnati Reds. Morgan would go on to win back-to-back NL MVP (Most Valuable Player) Awards, as Cincinnati went to the Fall Classic three of the next five seasons (1972, 1975-1976).

One of the players Houston received from Cincinnati was first baseman Lee May. In 1972, he led Houston to their first winning season (84-69). May clubbed a total of 81 homers in his 3 seasons with the Astros. He was then traded to Baltimore, where he led the American League (AL) with 109 RBIs in 1976.

Don Wilson's suicide in January 1975 was followed by the worst season in club history. The next year the Astros attempted to rebound under new management. J. R. Richard won 20 games for Houston in 1976. He followed that performance by leading the NL in strikeouts in 1978 (303) and 1979 (313).

Richard, along with veteran knuckle-baller Joe Niekro, headed the best pitching staff in baseball in 1979. Joe had 21 wins, which tied him for the league lead with his brother Phil Niekro, who pitched for the Atlanta Braves. Suddenly, the Astros were a team on the rise, finishing just 1.5 games behind the Reds in the NL West.

Entering 1980, the Houston Astros looked to put the disasters of the previous decade behind them. J. R. Richard made his first All-Star appearance that season. Then, while warming up in the season's second half, a blood clot formed in Richard's shoulder and found its way to his brain. The resulting stroke caused partial paralysis, ending the career of the powerful young pitcher. For Astro fans, it was one more painful tragedy they were forced to endure.

Facing page: In 1979, J.R. Richard led the NL in strikeouts with 313.

Express To The Stars

Despite the loss of J. R. Richard in 1980, the Astros' pitching staff remained the best in baseball. Joe Niekro completed his second consecutive 20-win season, leading Houston to their first NL West Division Title. Nolan Ryan joined the Astros that season after leading the AL in strikeouts seven times in the 1970s.

Ryan began his career in the NL as a relief pitcher for the New York Mets in 1966. He played eight seasons with the California Angels, where his 100-MPH (Miles Per Hour) fastball earned him the nickname, "The Ryan Express." The Astros made the Texas native Major League Baseball's first million-dollar man.

Another Hall-of-Fame bound Texan, Joe Morgan, also returned to play for Houston in 1980. He joined an offense powered by Jose Cruz and Cesar Cedeno. After putting together their finest season yet (93-70), the Astros nearly fell apart at the end.

Houston entered the final regular season series with a three-game lead over the Los Angeles Dodgers in the NL West. The Astros lost three straight to the Dodgers, finishing in a tie for first place. Joe Niekro picked up his 20th victory in a one-game playoff to salvage the division championship.

In their first National League Championship Series (NLCS), the Astros faced the Philadelphia Phillies. It was a best-of-five game set, in which four of the contests were decided in extra innings. Niekro pitched 10 scoreless innings in Game 3, allowing Houston to take a one game advantage in the series (2-1). The Phillies rallied to win the final two games and steal the NL Pennant from the Astros.

In 1981, the Astros outpitched the rest of the major leagues for the third straight season. Nolan Ryan was baseball's most difficult hurler to score upon, with an outstanding 1.69 earned run average (ERA). Ryan's fifth career no-hitter that season broke Sandy Koufax's previous major league record.

A players strike split the 1981 season into two halves. An unusual playoff format pitted the winners of each half-season to determine divisional champions. Houston finished with the best second-half record in the NL West. They were defeated by the Los Angeles Dodgers, winners of the first half.

For the next three seasons, Houston fell back in the standings. They continued to receive quality pitching from Nolan Ryan and Joe Niekro. Offensively, the Astros were struggling. Jose Cruz put together his finest season in 1983. Cruz led the NL in hits with 189, and finished third in the batting race with a .318 average.

Roger Craig was a pitching coach for the Houston Astros in 1978 and 1979. Craig became the guru of the "split-fingered fastball." Houston's Mike Scott became one of its finest practitioners.

Craig learned the pitch from its developer, the 1979 NL Cy Young Award winner, Bruce Sutter. The effectiveness of the "splitter" is a result of its deceptive quality. Appearing like a fastball to the hitter, the pitch drops off sharply as it crosses home plate. When Roger Craig began teaching the pitch to young prospects, the impact on baseball was immediate. Craig turned ordinary major league pitchers into 20-game winners. It became known as "the pitch of the 1980s."

Mike Scott won only 5 of his 29 starting assignments in 1984. After the season he contacted Roger Craig, who had recently retired from his post as pitching coach of the Detroit Tigers. Craig had already transformed Jack Morris into one of the top AL pitchers. He agreed to teach the "split-finger" pitch to the young Astro. Magically, Scott became an 18-game winner in 1985.

The next season, Mike Scott was the NL's Cy Young Award winner. He led the league in shutouts with five, and ERA with 2.22. His league-leading 306 strikeouts were nearly four times as many as he had struck out just two years earlier! Roger Craig, now managing the San Francisco Giants, watched from the dugout as Scott pitched a no-hitter against his team to clinch the 1986 NL West Division Title.

The Astros offense that season was bolstered by first baseman Glenn Davis. In his first full season, Davis became an NL All-Star. He had set an Astros rookie record in the previous season (1985), smashing 20 home runs. With 31 homers in 1986, Davis finished just behind Mike Schmidt for the league lead.

In the 1986 NLCS, the Houston Astros faced the New York Mets. The same two teams had entered the NL together 25 years earlier. In that time, the Mets had won two NL Pennants and a World Championship, while Houston had yet to appear in a Fall Classic. Two of the top pitching staffs in baseball went to battle in a best-of-seven series.

Mike Scott outdueled Dwight Gooden (1-0) in the series opener. A Glenn Davis homer was the only run scored in the game. It preserved a 5-hit shutout for Scott, who tied an NLCS record with 14 strikeouts. In Game 2, Nolan Ryan struck out 5 of the first 10 men he faced. The Mets rallied to knock him out of the game, and tied the series at a game apiece.

The Astros were up 5-4 in Game 3, when a two-run homer by New York's Lenny Dykstra won the game in the bottom of the ninth inning. Mike Scott returned for Game 4, allowing only three hits, to even the series for a second time (2-2).

Facing page: Mike Scott sends one of his rocket pitches to a San Francisco Giants batter in a 1986 game.

The final two games of the series were extra-inning affairs. In Game 5, Nolan Ryan allowed only 2 hits through 9 innings, while striking out 12. One of the hits was a solo shot by Darryl Strawberry, which tied the game 1-1. The Mets went on to victory (2-1) in the bottom of the 12th inning.

With New York leading the series three games to two, they needed a victory in Game 6 to avoid facing the red-hot Mike Scott for a third time. With two outs in the 16th inning, Houston's Kevin Bass struck out, leaving the winning run stranded on base. It was the longest post-season game in major league history. Mike Scott was voted the MVP of the series, but he never got a chance to pitch in Game 7. The New York Mets had their third NL Pennant in hand.

Mike Scott continued to have success over the next four seasons. But the Astros failed to return to the NLCS. In 1989, Scott's 20 wins led the NL. He retired in 1991.

In 1987, Nolan Ryan led the NL in strikeouts for the first time with 270. The Ryan Express also led the league with a 2.76 ERA. Somehow he won only half as many games as he lost, finishing with an 8-16 record. In his final season with the Astros in 1988, Ryan led the NL in strikeouts for the second straight time with 228. He joined the Texas Rangers in 1989, where he led the AL in strikeouts for the next two seasons. After whiffing his career 5,714th batter, Nolan Ryan retired in 1993. He is Major League Baseball's all-time strikeout king!

Keeping The Faith

As of 1995, the Houston Astros have yet to win their first NL Pennant. They have two NL West Division Championships to their credit. Of the 11 NLCS games in which they have participated, the Astros have lost four in extra innings. Houston recovered from the disasters of the 1970s to make the next decade their finest ever. Today, a corps of young stars are looking to launch the Astros to new heights.

Craig Biggio came to the major leagues for the first time in 1988. He has proven himself to be a versatile asset for the Houston ball club. Biggio was the NL's All-Star catcher in 1991. He returned to

Craig Biggio leaps in the air after forcing out Ryne Sandberg of the Chicago Cubs in a 1994 game. Biggio completed the throw for a double play. The Astros won 7-5.

the All-Star Game the following season as a second baseman. He is only the second player in major league history to make the transition from behind the plate to the field in an All-Star Game. Craig Biggio completed his finest season in 1995 (.302 batting average, 22 HRs, 33 stolen bases). His multiple abilities on the diamond may soon land him an MVP Award.

In 1994, Jeff Bagwell became the first Houston player to win the NL MVP Award. He was also the first Astro to be named NL Rookie of the Year when he won the award in 1991. If he remains healthy in 1996, Bagwell will play his first full season in four years. The power-hitting first baseman has yet to reach his full potential.

On September 8, 1993, Darryl Kile carried on the Texas tradition. Kile pitched a no-hit game to defeat the New York Mets 7-1. It was the ninth no-hitter in Astros' history. Darryl Kile and Shane Reynolds will lead Houston's young pitching staff into the future. Houston fans are keeping the faith, hoping their Astros will someday emerge as the World Champions of baseball!

Darryl Kile winds up to pitch in a 1994 game against the Florida Marlins.

Glossary

All-Star: A player who is voted by fans as the best player at one position in a given year.

American League (AL): An association of baseball teams formed in 1900 which make up one-half of the major leagues.

American League Championship Series (ALCS): A best-of-seven-game playoff with the winner going to the World Series to face the National League Champions.

Batting Average: A baseball statistic calculated by dividing a batter's hits by the number of times at bat.

Earned Run Average (ERA): A baseball statistic which calculates the average number of runs a pitcher gives up per nine innings of work.

Fielding Average: A baseball statistic which calculates a fielder's success rate based on the number of chances the player has to record an out.

Hall of Fame: A memorial for the greatest baseball players of all time located in Cooperstown, New York.

Home Run (HR): A play in baseball where a batter hits the ball over the outfield fence scoring everyone on base as well as the batter.

Major Leagues: The highest ranking associations of professional baseball teams in the world, currently consisting of the American and National Baseball Leagues.

Minor Leagues: A system of professional baseball leagues at levels below Major League Baseball.

National League (NL): An association of baseball teams formed in 1876 which make up one-half of the major leagues.

National League Championship Series (NLCS): A best-of-seven-game playoff with the winner going to the World Series to face the American League Champions.

Pennant: A flag which symbolizes the championship of a professional baseball league.

Pitcher: The player on a baseball team who throws the ball for the batter to hit. The pitcher stands on a mound and pitches the ball toward the strike zone area above the plate.

Plate: The place on a baseball field where a player stands to bat. It is used to determine the width of the strike zone. Forming the point of the diamond-shaped field, it is the final goal a base runner must reach to score a run.

RBI: A baseball statistic standing for *runs batted in.* Players receive an RBI for each run that scores on their hits.

Rookie: A first-year player, especially in a professional sport.

Slugging Percentage: A statistic which points out a player's ability to hit for extra bases by taking the number of total bases hit and dividing it by the number of at bats.

Stolen Base: A play in baseball when a base runner advances to the next base while the pitcher is delivering his pitch.

Strikeout: A play in baseball when a batter is called out for failing to put the ball in play after the pitcher has delivered three strikes.

Triple Crown: A rare accomplishment when a single player finishes a season leading their league in batting average, home runs, and RBIs. A pitcher can win a Triple Crown by leading the league in wins, ERA, and strikeouts.

Walk: A play in baseball when a batter receives four pitches out of the strike zone and is allowed to go to first base.

World Series: The championship of Major League Baseball played since 1903 between the pennant winners from the American and National Leagues.

Index